Anonymous

Some Facts about the Life and Public Services of Benjamin Helm Bristow, of Kentucky

Anonymous

Some Facts about the Life and Public Services of Benjamin Helm Bristow, of Kentucky

ISBN/EAN: 9783337063764

Printed in Europe, USA, Canada, Australia, Japan

Cover: Foto ©Raphael Reischuk / pixelio.de

More available books at **www.hansebooks.com**

SOME FACTS ABOUT

THE

LIFE AND PUBLIC SERVICES

OF

BENJAMIN HELM BRISTOW,

OF KENTUCKY.

DESIGNED AS A REPLY TO INQUIRIES OFTEN MADE RESPECTING THE LEADING
EVENTS OF HIS LIFE.

———————— ◆◆ ————————

NEW YORK:

EVENING POST STEAM PRESSES, 208 BROADWAY.

——
1876.

SOME FACTS ABOUT

THE

LIFE AND PUBLIC SERVICES

OF

BENJAMIN HELM BRISTOW,

OF KENTUCKY,

Designed as a reply to inquiries often made respecting the leading events of his career.

———————●●●———————

Benjamin Helm Bristow was born at Elkton, Todd Co., Kentucky, June 20, 1832. His father was Hon. Francis M. Bristow, a man of unspotted character, a distinguished lawyer and a member of the Constitutional Convention of Kentucky in 1850, and a representative in Congress in 1860–1. His grandfather was a baptist clergyman, a native of Virginia, and had served as a private soldier in the war of 1812. A great-uncle, from whom he derives his christian name, served in the army of the Revolution, and lost his life in the battle of Brandywine. The mother of Col. Bristow was a daughter of Richard Helm, of Hardin county, Kentucky, who belonged to one of the most prominent and honorable families of the State. Thus it appears that on both sides he comes of good stock. He has inherited superior qualities of mind and character. That he has done honor to a noble ancestry -the sequel abundantly proves.

ANTI-SLAVERY TRAINING.

It has been alleged that Col. Bristow is not to be trusted to carry out the principles of the Republican party because he was born in a slave-holding State. The suspicion thus cast upon him comes from those who risked nothing in becoming anti-slavery men, having merely drifted with the tide that swelled around them in the North after the passage of the Kansas-Nebraska Bill. So far as mere birthplace goes, Col. Bristow was born in the same neighborhood where Abraham Lincoln first saw the light, and both of them trace their ancestry backward through Virginia to good old English stock. Mr. Lincoln passed his younger years in Hardin county, Kentucky, and, as it happened, was a favorite and, in some sense, a protegé of Richard Helm, the grandfather of Col. Bristow on his mother's side. While the war was in-progress Col. Bristow had occasion to visit Washington City, and while there was presented to Mr. Lincoln. "Your name," said Mr. Lincoln, "is Benjamin *Helm* Bristow, is it not?" "It is, sir," replied Col. Bristow. "Let me give you a good shake of the hand then," added Mr. Lincoln ; " Your grandfather, Richard Helm, was very kind to me when I was a barefooted boy in Hardin county."

Col. Bristow's father and grandfather were both anti-slavery men in a slave-holding community. His father gave liberty to the slaves he had inherited from the relatives of his wife, and was noted for his efforts to ameliorate the condition of the colored people in his neighborhood. It is on record that, as a member of the Constitutional Convention of Kentucky, he voted against the clause in that instrument declaring the right of property in slaves to be as sacred as that of any other property. The Hon. James Speed, of Louisville, Mr. Lincoln's attorney-general, himself an anti-slavery man as far back as 1849, wrote to a friend under date May, 9, 1876, as follows concerning the secretary.

"I have known Mr. Bristow since his early manhood. His father and grandfather were emancipationist, so that by inheritance he was an anti-slavery man ; the principles so born in him have been carried out in his life.   *   *   *   *
All of his feelings, sympathies and convictions have been up and abreast with the enlightened sentiments of the times. The great principles of human freedom and equality before the law, which were born to the country in the four years' travail of Mr. Lincoln's administration, lay as close to the heart of Bristow as of any man, and in his place and according to his opportunities, he did all he could to establish and perpetuate them."

Both father and son were anti-slavery Whigs and followers of Henry Clay prior to the formation of the Republican party ; but Col. Bristow did not become a voter till 1853. In the following year the repeal of the Missouri Compromise took place, and he in common with the great body of the whig party opposed that fatal measure. But the spirit of slave propagandism was too strong in Kentucky to be successfully resisted. A few years later the Lecompton Bill came up in Congress, the object and intent of which was to force a pro-slavery constitution on the people of Kansas without their consent. The whig candidate for Governor of Kentucky, Hon. Joshua F. Bell, favored that measure, and the Bristows, father and son, refused to vote for him. They bolted the party ticket because they would not sanction a wicked measure intended to extend slavery and trample under foot the principle of self-government. Those who are able to recall the temper of the South on all measures affecting the "peculiar institution" between the years 1850 and 1860, need not to be told that it required uncommon steadfastness of principle to oppose, in a slaveholding community, any act which aimed to uphold and strengthen that institution. The Lecompton Bill, bad as it was, received the votes of eight Northern Senators and twenty-seven Northern Representatives No special merit is claimed for Col. Bristow that he placed himself in opposition to this measure, but it serves to show that his antagonism to slavery is no new-born zeal, that his political action was in harmony with that of the Republican party before the party had a well defined national existence, and that it was manifested in an atmosphere charged with the malaria which the actual presence of slavery breeds. Let any man who thinks that Col. Bristow is not to be trusted to carry out republican principles, ask himself what would probably have been his own political status twenty years ago, if he had been born and reared in a slave-holding State. He could not have sided with the republican sentiment of the country much earlier than Col. Bristow did. It will be shown hereafter that all of Col. Bristow's public acts have been consistent with his early opposition to the Lecompton infamy.

EDUCATION—PROFESSION—ENTRANCE TO THE ARMY.

In 1847 Mr. Bristow entered Jefferson College, Pennsylvania, from which he graduated in 1851, leaving behind him a reputation for solidity rather than brilliancy of scholarship. He was noted as a logical debater as well as for independence of character and sturdy, self reliant manhood. Returning to Elkton, he entered the law office of his father, where he studied two years. In 1853, he commenced the practice of law with success, remaining at Elkton till 1858, when he removed to Hopkinsville, Kentucky, and engaged in the practice of his profession there, in partnership with Judge R. J. Petree, and subsequently with the Hon. John Feland. Three years later the war of the rebellion commenced and Mr. Bristow promptly espousing the cause of the Union, announced his intention to enter the army. Kentucky was in a ferment, her wealth and aristocracy strongly in sympathy with the rebellion, and her old whig traditions still attaching her to the Union.

ARMY RECORD.

Col. Bristow was enrolled in the volunteer forces of the United States, September 20, 1861, and mustered in as lieutenant-colonel of the 25th Kentucky Infantry, at Calhoun, Ky., for the period of three years. Col. J. M. Shackleford was the commanding officer of the regiment, which was soon ordered to the front, and assigned to the army operating under Gen. Grant, on the Cumberland and Tennessee rivers. The regiment took part in the battle of Fort Donelson, where it displayed great gallantry, and lost heavily in officers and men. After the capture of the fort and the dispersion of the enemy the command was removed to Pittsburg Landing, where it was hotly engaged in the two days battle at that place. About an hour after the beginning of the engagement Col. Bristow was struck down by a shell which exploded near his head and rendered him insensible for the rest of the day. He was carried off the field, and for some time it was supposed that he would not revive. Major Wall, who then took command of the regiment, thus speaks of this incident in the report of the battle :

" About one hour after we had marched to the field occupied by us at the commencement of the engagement, the explosion

of a shell near and over Col. Bristow's head rendered him insensible the remainder of the day. His hearing is seriously,
and I fear permanently injured, and the spinal column is injured.
I had him removed from the field and took command of the
regiment."

When Col. Bristow recovered he made a report of that part of
the operation preceding the time when he was struck down,
and he thus refers to what happened to himself :

" After we had been on the ground about an hour an un-
fortunate accident occurred to me, which rendered me incapable of retaining command, and you are respectfully referred to
the report of Major Wall, who took command of this battalion
during the rest of the day."

The 25th regiment was so reduced in numbers by this and
previous engagements, that it was soon afterwards consolidated
with the 17th Kentucky, taking the name of the latter regiment.
By reason of the consolidation Col. Shackleford and Lieut.-Col.
Bristow returned home without delay and raised the 8th Kentucky Cavalry, which was mustered in for one year's service, at
Russellville, Ky., September 8, 1862. This regiment was one
of the finest in the West. The following facts are collated
from the report of the adjutant-general of Kentucky.

" The first battalion of this regiment was organized at Henderson, Ky., by Major Jas. H. Holloway. The second battalion
was organized by Col. Bristow at Russellville, Ky. The
third battalion was recruited at Lebanon, Ky., by Major J.
W. Weatherford. The whole regiment, numbering 1,248 men,
was recruited and organized within the space of three
weeks from the time authority was issued for the same, and
was composed of the very best material in the State. The
line officers were competent and gallant soldiers, and, from
the day of organization, their respective commands were well
disciplined and under perfect control. The first battalion,
under Major Holloway, commanded by· Col. Shackelford,
remained at Henderson, Ky., during the months of September and October, 1862, and were constantly skimishing
with the rebel forces under Adam Johnson. This battalion
together with one or two companies of Indiana cavalry, fought
a large force under Adam Johnson, at Geiger's Lake, and

scattered them in every direction. In this engagement Col Shackelford received a severe and painful wound while leading a charge."

The second and third battalions, in the meanwhile, were engaged in a number of skirmishes with the rebel Col. Woodward, and, finally, by a night march under Major Kennedy, they came upon his forces at Camp Coleman, in Todd county, Ky., dispersing the whole force."

"Upon the invasion of Kentucky by Bragg, Gen. Buell ordered the second and third battalions to join his command at Bowling Green, Ky. In conjunction with a part of the 4th Kentucky Cavalry they were assigned to the responsible duty of guarding Gen. Buell's immense wagon train across Green river. Upon returning to Bowling Green two companies of the 8th Cavalry were sent upon a scout into Tennessee, where they surprised and captured a party of over one hundred rebel soldiers who were engaged in collecting supplies for Bragg's army."

"In November, 1862, the first and second battalions were ordered to Russellville, Ky., and the third battalion ordered to Clarksville, Tenn., where it remained during the remainder of its term of enlistment, doing good service in repelling invasions and keeping open the Cumberland river, thus securing supplies to Gen. Rosecrans' army. During the winter and spring the first and second battalions were engaged in many skirmishes, and were assigned the duty of protecting the country west of the Nashville Railroad."

· "In January, 1863, Col. Shackelford was promoted Brigadier-General, and Lieut. Col. B. H. Bristow was commissioned Colonel."

"This regiment and a battalion of the 3d Kentucky Cavalry, under command of Col. Bristow, were in pursuit of Morgan in his raid through Kentucky, Indiana and Ohio, and did good service in that long and fatiguing march, and were present at the taking of the notorious raider."

"The regiment was mustered out of service at Russellville, Ky., September 23d, 1863."

Gen. Schackelford commanding the brigade in which the 8th Kentucky Cavalry served, in his report of the capture of Morgan, thus speaks of the conduct of Col. Bristow :

"It is difficult for me to speak of individual officers or men without doing injury to others. I unhesitatingly bear testimony to the uniform good conduct and gallant bearing of the whole command. Yet I cannot forbear to mention the names of some of the officers * * Col. Bristow, Lieut. Col. Holloway and Maj. Starling of the 8th Kentucky * * * deserve the gratitude of the whole country for their energy and gallantry."

IN THE STATE SENATE.

On New Year's day, 1863, President Lincoln issued his Proclamation of Emancipation. This document produced intense excitement in Kentucky, and a movement was set on foot by some of the so-called Unionists of the State, under the leadership of Gov. Wickliffe, to resist it. In the following August, while serving in the field, Col. Bristow was elected to the State Senate from Todd and Christian counties, in opposition to the Wickliffe movement. The peril to the State from the sudden defection of a large number of those who had hitherto espoused the Union cause was imminent, for if Kentucky should, at this critical hour, join the rebellion, the consequences both to herself and to the nation, would be likely to prove most disastrous. The neighbors and friends of Col. Bristow called him back from the field to meet this new danger. It has been alleged that he resigned from the army because he was not willing to serve with colored troops. The truth is that he did not resign at all. He was mustered out with his regiment at the expiration of their term of service. Colored troops had not then been called into the service, but when they were, Col. Bristow heartily approved of the step, declaring that he would use every instrument that Providence had placed in our hands to quench the fires of secession, and to maintain the unity of the nation.

In the winter of 1863, Col. Bristow attended a meeting of the anti-slavery men of Kentucky, to devise means to bring the State into harmony with the principles of the Emancipation Proclamation by repealing the laws which required free negroes to leave the State, and which made every person who assisted a slave to obtain his freedom, liable to criminal prosecution. At this meeting Col. Bristow took the most advanced ground, and by his clear-sighted and undaunted course elicited the high encomiums of the venerable and loyal Robert J. Breckinridge, who has borne, for a quarter of a century, one of the most honored names in the Presbyterian church of the United States.

MEASURES FOR SUPPRESSING THE REBELLION.

If any better proof can be required of Col. Bristow's fidelity to the Union and to the anti- slavery principles in which he was nurtured than his willingness to shed his blood in their defense, his record as a member of the Kentucky Legislature furnishes it in ample measure. The period of his service in that body embraces not only the ordinary steps taken to suppress the rebellion, but the more important one of acting upon the thirteenth amendment to the Constitution. His term of service commenced on the 7th December, 1863, when he was less than thirty-two years of age. In a very short while, however, he was recognized as the leader of the Union men in that branch of the Legislature, and the ablest debater in either party. His previous services in the field as an officer in the Union army, gave him a thorough knowledge, not only of the wants of the soldiers, but of the strength of the rebellion.

We propose now to trace his record in the Legislature of a State which was regarded with universal suspicion by the friends of the Government during the war for the suppression of the rebellion.

Early in the session of the Kentucky Senate, a resolution was offered directing the sergeant-at-arms " to procure and cause to be raised in front of the State Capitol a suitable banner, with stars and stripes," during the sitting of the General Assembly. Bristow voted for that resolution. (*Ky. Sen., Journal*, 1863-4, *pp.* 32-3.)

On the 14th January, 1864, the Kentucky Senate took up for consideration a bill authorizing the Governer of the State to raise a force not exceeding 5,000, men, to " be used for State defense against guerrillas and guerrilla raids, and for such other military services against the rebel armies and troops as may be necessary," and also " to co-operate with the Federal forces within Kentucky." The bill proposed that the troops be raised " by volunteering or by draft." The " draft " feature was not agreeable to the Southern members of the Kentucky Senate, and one of them moved to strike out the words " or by draft." Bristow voted against the motion to strike out, and, after it was rejected, voted for the bill. (*Ky. Sen. Journal*, 1863-4 *pp*. 139, 140.)

About the same time an interesting incident occurred in the Kentucky Legislature with reference to the 4th and 6th Kentucky Cavalry Regiments, whose original terms of service had expired in January, 1864. They re-enlisted as veterans, and were at Louisville, Kentucky, without having been paid for the previous two months.

To meet the emergency, a resolution was offered in the Kentucky Legislature, acknowledging their gallant achievements and exalted patriotism, and directing the auditor to draw his warrant upon the treasurer for $20,000, " to pay off these gallant men," specifying that the sum was advanced for the use of the Government and to be disbursed by the U. S. Paymaster under the regulations of the War Department.

Among those who voted for that resolution was B. H. Bristow. (*Ky. Sen. Journal*, 1863-4 *pp*. 188-9-90.)

During the first session of Col. Bristow's term as a member of the Kentucky Senate, there was a widely extended combination in the State to excite the people to acts of open hostility against the Government of the United States. For the purpose of defeating this combination a bill was reported to the Kentucky Senate, the provisions of which were intended to punish treasonable and disloyal practices.

The bill provided that any person aiding, encouraging or inducing any officer, soldier or guerrilla of the so-called Confederate States, to destroy or injure property in Kentucky, or to injure, arrest, kidnap or otherwise maltreat any citizen or resident of Kentucky, or any person who should aid, harbor or conceal such guerrillas, or confederate soldiers, should be guilty of a high misdemeanor, and, upon conviction, be subject to fine and imprisonment. It further provided that speaking or writing against the Government of the United States, or in favor of the Confederate States, or any wilful endeavor to excite insurrection or rebellion, or to terrify or prevent the people of Kentucky from supporting and maintaining the Federal

Government, should be punishable by fine and imprisonment Similar penalties were prescribed against failure to give information of raids or approach of guerrillas. Also special provisions were made in this bill that any attorney at law who violated the oath prescribed by the State Constitution should be forever debarred from practicing law in the State of Kentucky.

The record shows B. H. Bristow as voting for this bill in all its stages. (Ky. Senate Journal, 1863-4, pp. 333-4).

As a corollary to the foregoing bill, Col. Bristow gave his vote and voice to the support of a bill entitling any person injured by guerrillas or armed bands not acting under the authority of the United States or the State of Kentucky, to recover such damages for personal injuries as a jury should find, and for property injured or destroyed, to recover double the value thereof. A provision of peculiar stringency, demanded by the necessities of the time and locality was made, imposing a liability in damages for all illegal acts done by such guerrillas or predatory bands in any county of Kentucky upon any disloyal person having knowledge of the presence of such band, within the county of his residence, who failed to give immediate information thereof to the civil or military authorities in such county.

The second section of said bill provided that evidence of the loyalty or disloyalty of the defendant should be admissible, as well as the previous character for loyalty or disloyalty of those committing said acts of depredation, who were not sued. (*Ibid*, pp. 413-414). A Democrat moved to amend the bill by adding a proviso making the test of loyalty of a defendant to be the adherence to and support of the Constitution of the United States and of the State Kentucky, and compliance with laws enacted in pursuance thereof. This proviso was so manifest an endeavor to impair the efficacy of the act, that Col. Bristow, with other Republicans, earnestly resisted its embodiment in the bill. It was approved, however, by a majority, and became law. (Ky. Senate Journal, 1863-4, p. 415).

Significant proof of Colonel Bristow's fidelity to the maintenance of the Union is furnished by his vote upon a measure to make disposition of the stock in the Southern Bank of Kentucky owned by the State. On the 15th February, 1864, a bill came up for consideration in the Kentucky Senate, which, as reported, empowered the Commissioners of the Sinking Fund to sell the coin, realized from the sale of the stock, for United States currency, to pay the banks of the State any portion of the military loan due said banks by the State, and to invest the balance in Kentucky State bonds, the bonds of the United States known as 5-20 bonds, or other government securities.

A Southern rights democrat, true to his instincts and desires, moved to strike out the words "the bonds of the United States known as 5-20 bonds or other government securities." Colonel Bristow opposed this amendment by his vote, and supported the bill as reported. (Ky. Senate Journal, 1863-4, pp. 379-80).

The resolutions offered by Gen. W. C. Whitaker, on the 20th February, 1864, in the Kentucky Senate, acknowledging the gallantry, bravery and efficiency of the soldiers and officers from that State, and tendering to them and to the officers and soldiers of sister States the merited tribute of thanks for their fortitude and endurance of the hardships of war, was opposed by the democrats, but secured the earnest advocacy of Colonel Bristow.

THE THIRTEENTH AMENDMENT.

An attempt has been made in certain quarters to misrepresent the position of Colonel Bristow in reference to the 13th amendment to the Constitution. But his record is entirely clear upon that subject. On the 7th February, 1865, the governor of Kentucky communicated to the State Senate an attested copy of the joint resolution of Congress, proposing the 13th amendment to the Constitution, abolishing and prohibiting slavery in the United States. On the 22d of February, 1865, the Kentucky Senate proceeded to consider the resolutions reported by the majority of the committee to whom the proposed 13th amendment had been referred, proposing the rejection of said amendment. (Ky. Senate Journal, 1865, pp. 387-8). On the same day Senator Fisk offered a substitute, wherein, after reciting the requisite action on said amendment by Congress, and its submission to the States for ratification, it provided as follows :

" 1. *Resolved* by the General Assembly of the commonwealth of Kentucky, That the proposed amendment of the Constitution of the United States, above recited, be, and it is hereby, ratified by this Legislature.

" 2. *Resolved*, That, recognizing the fact that the rebellion and the measures of the government necessary for its suppression have practically destroyed property in slaves, we deem it proper that loyal men, who have not participated in that rebellion, nor given it aid or comfort, should be compensated for their losses thus sustained, and we request our senators and representatives in Congress to urge that such compensation be made ; but, relying with full confidence upon the justice of our government, and making no reservations in the performance of what we believe the true interest and safety of our country demand at our hands, we declare this, our solemn act of ratification, to be absolute and without conditions." (Kentucky Senate Journal, 1865, p. 388).

Twelve senators voted for the substitute, and among the members was Benjamin H. Bristow.

Senator Robinson then moved, as a substitute, a bill providing that upon the payment by the government of the United States to the State of Kentucky, for the use of its citizens, the owners of slaves therein, thirty-six millions five hundred and thirty thousand four hundred and ninety-six dollars (the assessed value of slaves for taxation in 1864), as compensation for slaves enlisted or drafted into the Federal army and for damage sustained by such slave-owners by violation of their claims to the labor and service of their slaves and for all claims on account of their emancipation, then and thenceforth slavery should be prohibited in Kentucky, and all laws concerning slaves be repealed, marriages of slaves be legal, &c., and upon such payment being made, " then and thenceforth the General Assembly doth ratify said 13th amendment to the Constitution of the United States ; and the governor is directed to make proclamation of such ratification upon such payment being made."

All slaves emancipated by the proposed act, however, were required to remove from the State within ten years of their emancipation, and if the conditions of the proposed act (as to payment, &c.,) were not accepted and complied with on the part of the government of the United States on or before 1st January, 1866, then and in that event Kentucky absolutely rejected and refused to ratify said amendments.

(Kentucky Senate Journal, 1865, pp. 389-90.)

Senator Landrum moved to add to the second section of Senator Robinson's amendment these words: "except the second section of said article, which is hereby rejected." Senator Bristow voted against Landrum's motion, but the motion prevailed. Senator Bristow then voted against Robinson's substitute as amended, and finally voted against the report of the committee. On the 24th of February he voted against the preamble and resolutions passed by the Kentucky House of Representatives, rejecting the amendment, which had been sent to the Senate for concurrence.

We thus find Col. Bristow, eleven years ago, while the war was still in progress, voting in a slave-holding State for the unconditional ratification of the 13th amendment, going farther, in fact, than Mr. Lincoln had gone, since the latter proposed and favored compensation to the loyal owners of slaves for the loss of their property.

A sample of democratic statesmanship will be seen in the bill concerning slaves and runaways, offered in the Kentucky Senate on the 25th of February, 1865, viz.:

"SECTION 1. Be it enacted by the General Assembly of the Commonwealth of Kentucky, That all laws now in force in this Commonwealth requiring the owner of a slave to pay a reward for the arrest or apprehension of such slave as a runaway, be and the same are hereby repealed.

"SEC. 2. That any person who hereafter shall, without the consent of the owner, hire or permit to remain in his or her service the negro slave of any other person, that the person so hiring or permitting to remain in his or her service such slave, shall be liable to the owner thereof for the sum of five dollars for every twenty-four hours such slave may be in such service, to be recovered and collected as other debts for similar amounts under existing laws. Any judgment under this section may be enforced by execution of *ca. sa.*

"SEC. 3. That the owner of a slave may, by his written permission and authority, license and permit his slave to act as the agent of the owner, and hire himself or herself out for the benefit of the master, or that of the slave, if so expressed. The terms owner and master in this act mean the person entitled to the possession and control of the slave.

"SEC. 4. Be it further enacted, That it shall be the duty of all sheriffs, marshals, policemen, and other ministerial peace officers, and it shall be the right of all other persons, to arrest all negro slaves fit for, and who will be received into, the military service of the United States, whom they may find going at large, without the written permit of the master of such slave, and not engaged in the business of the master; and such slave so arrested shall be, by the person arresting him, taken and put into the military service of the United States, to be credited to the county of his owner's residence.

"SEC. 5. For each negro so arrested and put into the service of the United States the person arresting and delivering him shall receive the sum of twenty dollars, to be paid out of the State Treasury upon his production to the auditor of the certificate of the proper officer of the United States showing the delivery and reception thereof;

" Provided, however, that when any negro arrested under this act shall be willing and request to return to his master or owner, then the arrester shall take and deliver such slave to the master or owner, who shall pay to the arrester the sum of twenty dollars and the reasonable costs and expenses incurred after the arrest and in so returning such slave.

" Provided, That no such enlistment shall be made into the army, under this act, without the consent of the master of such slave." (Senate Journal, 1865, 429 to 431).

Against this bill, in all its stages, Bristow, with the little band of republican senators, voted.

At the same session of the Kentucky Senate there was another vote, which indicated the state of feeling in Kentucky. At that time there existed at Berea, in Madison county, Kentucky, a church and school under the control of certain Abolitionists, who recognized no distinctions, political or otherwise, based on color. In the church and in the school, whites and blacks mingled, much to the disgust of Kentuckians who had been reared under the influence of slavery, and the Virginia and Kentucky resolutions of 1798. The brethren at Berea desired an act of incorporation for their little church, and to that end a bill was presented to the Kentucky Senate proposing to incorporate " Rev. John G. Fee, Teman Thomson and Morgan Burdett" and their successors, a body politic and corporate, "for the church of Christ at Berea, Madison county, Kentucky." The proposed charter contained nothing of a political or sectarian nature, and granted nothing but the usual powers incident to all such corporations. But the Kentucky Senate could not tolerate the Fee sect, and denied to the Berea abolitionists a simple act of incorporation for church purposes. Among those who voted for the resolution was Benjamin H. Bristow.

During the year 1864 Col. Bristow was engaged in the practice of law at Louisville and Hopkinsville, and in the intervals of professional and senatorial labor he took an earnest part in the presidential canvass, making speeches and using his great personal influence to secure the election of Mr. Lincoln. He supported the president in all his measures for the re-establishment of the Union, and whether in the senate or on the stump, he earnestly advocated the adoption of all the amendments to the Constitution.

UNITED STATES DISTRICT ATTORNEY FOR KENTUCKY.

The war having ended and many of the great questions having been settled, Col. Bristow resigned his seat in the Senate of Kentucky in 1865, and removed to Louisville, where he entered upon the practice of his profession. In the following year he was appointed U. S. district attorney for Kentucky. The duties of this position were extremely arduous. The rebel element had returned from the war and the pro-slavery faction of the State, including those who had taken refuge temporarily in Canada and elsewhere, had organized numerous Ku Klux bands to harass and murder the freedmen and white Unionists. A reign of terror was inaugurated which could be extinguished only by the civil power of the Government, acting through the courts of law. Col. Bristow threw himself into this work with all the energy of his nature, and so zealously did he pursue the lawless bands that were patrolling the State, that during his term of office he procured twenty-nine convictions before Kentucky juries for various crimes under the Enforcement Act, from common assault to willful murder, and was only stopped at last by a decision of the Supreme Court of the United States declaring that the court below had no jurisdiction of

2

that class of offenses. This decision was made in the case of the United States *vs.* Blyew, the legal aspects of which will be more particularly referred to hereafter. John Blyew and George Kennard had been indicted and tried by Col. Bristow for the murder of a whole family of colored persons. The case caused great excitement in Kentucky, and when the jury brought in a verdict of guilty of murder in the first degree the Ku Klux fraternity were stricken with terror, not merely in Kentucky but throughout the whole South. Sentence of death was pronounced upon the prisoners, but they took an appeal to the Supreme Court with the result already stated.

Among the convictions obtained by Col. Bristow was that of a wealthy Kentuckian who, shortly after the ratification of the 13th Amendment, gave a brutal whipping to a negro woman named Rose Ann McIlroy, whom he claimed as a slave. Col. Bristow caused him to be indicted in the Federal Court. This was something entirely novel in the annals of Kentucky, and when it was found that the indictment was serious and that the case would surely be tried, great efforts were made by the friends of the culprit to get the case dismissed. Among others who visited Louisville for this purpose was a distinguished member of Congress. This gentleman called upon Col. Bristow and said that one of his neighbors, a very respectable man, had got into trouble and been indicted. "For what offense?" asked Col. Bristow. "O, he only flogged a negro woman," was the answer. "Flogged a woman!" exclaimed Col. Bristow, "then, without knowing the particulars, I should say he ought to be hanged." This was the only satisfaction given to the member of Congress for his respectable constituent. But the efforts of the indicted party and his friends did not end here. Delegations of respectable people came forward and long petitions were prepared and signed, setting forth the good character of the accused. Col. Bristow stood firm and declared his intention to make an example of a woman-whipper, and to prosecute every case of this kind brought to his notice to the last extremity. The offender was committed. Col. Bristow then instituted a civil action for damages and secured a judgment for the sum of one thousand dollars in behalf of the colored woman who had been so outrageously maltreated. The money was collected and paid over to her. It is believed that a more vigorous and successful effort was made in Kentucky to carry out the Enforcement Act than in any other State in the Union, and this was entirely due to Col. Bristow's personal and professional efforts to protect the colored people.

During the same period of time the practice of illicit distillation was rife in Kentucky, though not to so great an extent as it has been in some of the Northern States. This was due to the fact that the whiskey of that region being of a finer quality, mainly used for drinking purposes, required to be stored for a year before being ready for the market, and thus afforded a better opportunity to the government officers for the detection of fraud connected with it. Col. Bristow attacked the whiskey rings there with the same vigor he has displayed as Secretary of the Treasury, and during his term of office as District Attorney secured one hundred and one forfeitures of separate lots of distilled spirits, ranging from two barrels up to two hundred each, besides machinery and implements for producing it.

BRISTOW AND RECONSTRUCTION.

It will be remembered that when Andrew Johnson first showed signs of a reactionary policy, many of the leading Republican statesmen, including Mr. Morton of Indiana, and Mr. Fessenden of Maine, sustained him for a considerable time, conceiving that the best interests of the Republican party required that they should not come to a rupture with him till his purposes were more fully disclosed. While matters were in this shape Mr. Johnson made an attempt to capture the federal officeholders in all parts of the country and commit them to his intended policy. Col. Bristow was then District Attorney of Kentucky, and a persistent attempt was made to entrap him with the other Kentucky officers. At a soldiers' convention, where he was present, Governor Bramlette took occasion to introduce a resolution endorsing the policy of Andrew Johnson. Col. Bristow immediately arose and offered to amend by adding the words—"Understanding it to be the fixed and cherished policy of his lamented predecessor Abraham Lincoln." In support of his amendment he said:

" No man in this country had more of my love, respect and veneration than Mr. Lincoln. If we must have Mr. Johnson's name in the resolution let us have Mr. Lincoln's too. If, as I understand Mr. Johnson, he is carrying out the policy of Mr. Lincoln, I am for Mr. Johnson. With this express understanding I indorse Mr. Johnson, but I will not indorse him in the language of every rebel meeting in Kentucky, nor in the way of those who, while they endorse him, reassert the fundamental and originating principles of the rebellion, the abominable and infamous resolutions of '98."

SOLICITOR-GENERAL OF THE UNITED STATES.

Col. Bristow resigned the office of District Attorney Jan. 1, 1870, and formed a law partnership with Gen. John M. Harlan of Louisville. Shortly afterwards Congress passed a statute changing the old Attorney-General's office into the Department of Justice, and creating a second high law officer to assist the Attorney-General in its administration, called the Solicitor-General. To this office Colonel Bristow was appointed in October, 1870, and he held it until after General Grant's re-election in 1872. During the absences of the Attorney-General from Washington he acted as head of the department, and at other times was principally employed in writing opinions on questions of law submitted to the Department of Justice by the other departments of government, and in the argument of causes in the Supreme Court. His discharge of the onerous duties that devolved upon him was marked by the conscientious, pains-taking industry, the courtesy, the firmness, the independence and the hatred of fraud and chicanery which have distinguished his entire public life, but besides this he gained a brilliant repu-tation by the ability he displayed in arguments in court. The judges of the court at once recognized him as one of the ablest men who appeared before them and have ever spoken of his great services to them in the assistance which his arguments gave them. Besides the ordinary revenue and claims cases, many cases of great constitutional importance were then before the court, in arguing which Mr. Bristow took the leading part. Among these were cases involving the constitutionality of the Confiscation and Enforcement Acts, the effect of a pardon on the status of persons guilty of rebellion, and the jurisdiction of the Circuit Court to try crimes against persons of the colored race. The latter question arose in the case previously mentioned, of The United States vs. Blyew, reported in volume 13 of Wallace's Reports. Some Ku Klux ruffians murdered a colored family under circumstances of such unprovoked and wanton cruelty that they were in great danger of being lynched. As the law of Kentucky then was they could not be tried in the State courts, because all the witnesses were colored people, and a colored man could not be a witness against a white. Col. Bristow who was then District Attorney for Kentucky, had them indicted, tried and convicted under the Enforcement Act in the United States Circuit Court. The case being brought by writ of error to the Supreme Court at Washington, he argued the case as Solicitor-General against Judge Black and Mr. Isaac Caldwell, a distinguished lawyer of Kentucky, and urged with great force and eloquence the legality of the proceedings in the court below. A majority of the court felt compelled, although they came to this conclusion with great reluctance, to decide that the Circuit Court had no jurisdiction, and therefore to reverse judgment. As the State of Kentucky assumed the prosecution of the writ of error, Col. Bristow was thus placed in a position of antagonism to his native State which caused some bitter remarks to be made against him by fellow-Kentuckians, but indignation at the crime and at the cruel injustice of the Kentucky statute, that allowed it to go unpunished, more than overcame any reluctance he might otherwise have had to resist the claim of the State to exclusive jurisdiction of all such offenses committed within her border.

One marked characteristic of Mr. Bristow's arguments was an absence of all attempt at display. He always thoroughly prepared himself, going over every case in which he did not make the brief, with as much care as if nothing had been done in its preparation, and making voluminous notes and memoranda. But when he came to speak he would never make any further use of these than the posture of the case demanded; and if he thought the case had been sufficiently argued by his associate, would add but a few remarks on one or two of the most vital points. The great judgment he thus showed in arguing the important questions and leaving the others alone, and never unnecessarily taking up the time of the overworked judges, was one reason why he was so great a favorite with them, and was always listened to with respectful attention. In this connection it is proper to state that several members of the Supreme Court have been heard to say that they regarded him as one of the soundest lawyers in the country. His mind and tendencies are eminently judicial, and it is well known that his name was amongst those considered both by the Court and the President for the vacancy in the supreme bench caused by the death of Chief Justice Chase and by the retirement o Justice Nelson. With his associates in the department he was extremely popular, being always frank and cordial in his intercourse with them, and generously avoiding taking the credit of work to himself that he thought belonged to them.

HIS VIEWS ON NEGRO TESTIMONY.

The decision of the Supreme Court in the case of Blyew prompted Col. Bristow to renewed efforts 'to remove the disqualifications of colored men as witnesses in the courts of Kentucky. In a speech, in Louisville, in July, 1871, he presented his views on negro testimony, in the following language :

" Turning from the Constitution to the statute book, we find there provisions which no thoughtful man will defend, but which the Democratic Legislature has persistently refused to modify. Since slavery was abolished by the operation of the thirteenth amendment to the Constitution of the United States, the Legislature of Kentucky has been in the hands of the Democratic party. If any intelligent foreigner, who was ignorant of the events that have transpired in this country within the past ten years, should be called upon to look over the present Constitution and statute laws of Kentucky, he could come to no other conclusion than that African slavery still exists in this State. Turn to the statute regulating homestead exemption and testimony, and the laws relating to the subject of education, and no sane man can fail to perceive that, if slavery be actually dead, the spirit of the 'departed' still lingers in Kentucky, and controls her law-makers. The statute of Kentucky, which denies to 225,000 colored people of the

State the right to testify in any case, civil or criminal, affecting a white person, has its origin in the supposed necessities of slavery, and is indefensible in a land of freedom. This denial is a monstrous and grievous wrong to both races. It is a practical denial of freedom to the colored race; yea, it is even worse than that; it is a license, if not an invitation, to base miscreants and cowardly Ku Klux to gratify their brutal passions and satiate their murderous propensities on this unoffending and defenceless race. For the credit of my own State I do not choose to dwell on the horrors that have disgraced many parts of this Commonwealth since the abolishment of slavery, nearly all of which are traceable directly to the criminal refusal of the Legislature to treat the negro as a human being, entitled to the protection of law. Civilization has now progressed too far to require argument to prove the monstrosity of the denial of this right, which is absolutely essential to the freedom and personal security of every man. No intelligent man will attempt to justify the action, or, rather, I should say, the non-action of the Legislature in this regard; and yet the platform of the Democratic party commits this subject to the 'tomb of the Capulets,' and refuses to pledge itself to correct this fearful evil. I said no intelligent man would now justify this course; perhaps this statement should be qualified. There are men in Kentucky—and the species is peculiar to Kentucky—who seem to be sane, and may be called intelligent on every subject except the negro, but when he is introduced they become as 'mad as March hares.' They tell us it is right to et the negro testify in all cases; that the highest interest of society demands it; but, say they, Congress transcended its constitutional power in passing its 'civil-rights bill,' and therefore we will not modify the Kentucky statute. Reducing this so-called argument to a plain syllogistic statement, it amounts to this: Congress did wrong, and therefore we ought not to do right. A twelve-year old lad, who would deduce such a conclusion from such premises, would be in danger of the rod in any log school-house outside Kentucky."

"But it cannot be admitted that Congress did wrong in passing the civil rights bill. Without stopping here to defend this act, I only say, that if Congress, after having taken part in the emancipation of the negro, had not passed some such act to secure his freedom, and give him the means of vindicating his rights in States where all such means were withheld, it would have been unfaithful to duty, and justly censurable in the estimation of the civilized world."

RESIGNS POSITION OF SOLICITOR-GENERAL.

In the autumn of 1872, it having become known that Colonel Bristow intended to resign the office of Solicitor-General, which he had held under both Mr. Ackerman and Mr. Geo. H. Williams, Col. Thomas A. Scott offered him the position of attorney for the Texas & Pacific Railway Company, which he accepted. Before he had entered upon his new duties he was asked also to accept the position of president of the California & Texas Construction Company.

As soon as his resignation was accepted by the President, Col. Bristow entered upon the duties of his new position, understanding that they were to be mainly professional and administrative. After several months' service, he realized that in this respect he was mistaken, and that his duties were coming to be largely non-professional. He therefore tendered his resignation, and after some delay it was accepted, and he resumed the practice of law at Louisville. During his connection with this enterprise, the financial management, including the sale of its securities, was solely under the control of Col. Scott. Col. Bristow never undertook to place any of them, nor was it his duty to do so. No man ever invested a dollar in the bonds or stock of the Texas & Pacific Railway, or of any corporation connected with it, by his advice or procurement; but even if he had sold all of these securities, conscientiously believing them to be sound and safe, no blame could have attached to him. He had nothing whatever to do with the procurement of the charters and land grants of the undertaking, and has never taken any part in advancing its interest since he severed his official connection with it. It is true that when he first accepted employment by the Texas & Pacific Railway Company, he bought a small interest in its securities, paying par in cash; but immediately after his nomination as Attorney-General, and before the action of the Senate was known in reference to the nomination of Geo. H. Williams, as Chief Justice, upon which his own confirmation necessarily depended, feeling that as a public officer he could not afford to hold an interest in any undertaking which might become an applicant for Government aid, he directed a friend in New York to sell his securities for whatever they would bring, and this was done at less than fifteen per cent. of their original cost. This is the end and extent of his connection with the Texas & Pacific Railway.

NOMINATED ATTORNEY-GENERAL.

For a week or ten days previous to December 1st, 1873, Col. Bristow had been mentioned frequently as one whom the President was thinking of inviting to his cabinet. Col. Bristow was then quietly practicing law in Louisville, and neither he nor his friends were seeking any appointment for him. The frequent newspaper announcements annoyed him, and on December 1, 1873, the very day that his nomination as Attorney-General was determined upon in Washington he wrote to a friend as follows:

" Would you do me the favor to ask your and my friends in Newspaper Row to quit sending dispatches to the effect that I am likely to be appointed to office?

" I am quietly pursuing my profession here—am not a candidate for any office, and it is not at all likely that any one will be offered me. It is not pleasant to be understood as a standing candidate for any vacant office, and besides it does not help a lawyer to have it often announced that he will probably withdraw from practice. I am grateful to my friends for thinking of me in connection with high office, but as it is not probable that one who is not seeking office will get it, I hope they will spare me the mortification of frequent defeats and disappointments. "

The appointment of Attorney-General Williams as Chief Justice of the Supreme Court not having been confirmed by the Senate, the expected vacancy in the former office did not occur, and Colonel Bristow's nomination was accordingly withdrawn.

SECRETARY OF THE TREASURY.

On the retirement of Mr. Richardson from the Treasury Department, the President appointed Col. Bristow to the highest administrative position in his gift, that of Secretary of the Treasury, June 3, 1874, and here he has won his greatest distinction. Advanced to a position of larger powers and more commanding influence, he soon attracted the attention and won the plaudits of the public by the reforms he introduced in the general administration of the office, as well as the vigor he displayed in enforcement of the laws for the collection of the revenue.

One of the first acts of Col. Bristow after his accession to the Treasury Department was to suppress the wasteful functionary holding the office of supervising architect. This individual had grown from small beginnings to be a perfect cormorant in his appetite for appropriations; his demands upon the public purse for architectural and decorative exploits reaching some ten millions per annum. The outrages upon good taste and ordinary business principles perpetrated by the supervising architect had become so notorious and exasperating, and withal so chronic, that he seemed to constitute a "ring" within himself, almost as powerful as the whiskey ring. He and his friends, the contractors for erecting and furnishing public buildings, were almost as much astounded, when they found he was out of office, as though the earth had been struck by a comet. Simultaneously with the suppression of Mullett, Secretary Bristow suspended all work on buildings not required by the public interests, and issued orders to discontinue the style of oriental magnificence in furniture and decoration which had been inaugurated by the former regime.

The Secretary next turned his attention to the corrupt and scoundrelly gang of so-called detectives in the Treasury Department, of whom Whitley, the Washington safe burglar, was chief. He dismissed this gang and called to the service Mr. Elmer Washburn, the admirable ex-superintendent of police in Chicago, whose efforts in the way of reform in that city had so roused the ire of local politicians (who have since pleaded guilty to indictments for whiskey frauds), that he was driven from his position there. Mr. Washburn has vindicated the wisdom of Secretary Bristow's choice not only by most important services in the crooked whiskey war, but by such vigorous and successful assaults on counterfeiters that the price of counterfeit money has risen from twenty cents on the dollar—the figure at which it was formerly furnished by the manufacturers—to eighty cents, the present quotation. The cost and risk of counterfeiting have been increased four-fold since Secretary Bristow came into office.

The Secretary found that the office of the second Comptroller of the Treasury was so loosely managed that it had ceased to be any real check upon dishonest and fraudulent claims, and that the Comptroller himself, in the capacity of member of the Board of Audit for the District of Columbia, had allowed claims upon the Treasury for more than five million dollars in excess of the amount contemplated and authorized by law. When this state of facts was discovered the Secretary sent the Comptroller and his principal subordinates to travel the same road with Mullett and Whitley.

By the consolidation of collection districts, both in the customs and internal revenue service, and the discharge of surplus officials and machinery, Secretary Bristow has saved to Government between three and four million dollars per annum, besides rendering the service itself more efficient. For, with the consolidation of districts, the collectors and their subordinates have ceased to stand in fear of their immediate representatives in Congress. Their field has been enlarged, and their political independence increased. Many instances might be cited of the improved efficiency of the services, traceable to this small dose of civil service reform.

The smugglers in and around the New York Custom House were next attacked vigorously and successfully, and an end put to the erroneous an systematic frauds in the importation of silks. A thorough overhauling of the New Orleans Custom House followed, and savings were effected there to the amount of over eighty thousand dollars per annum.

Since Secretary Bristow's accession to office the sum of $178,548,300 of the six per cent. bonds of the United States have been refunded into five per cent. bonds at par, at the unprecedentedly low cost of one-half of one per cent. commissions; the parties subscribing for the bonds paying all cost of transmitting the five per cents to London and the six per cents to Washington, making the real cost of the negotiation to the Government equal to a commission of about one-quarter of one per cent. Under this arrangement all the five per cents authorized by law have been disposed of, and a saving of five millions per annum in gold interest effected. The Secretary believes that a four and a half per cent. bond, having thirty years to run, can now or soon be negotiated at par, at no higher cost to the Government than that paid for negotiating the last installment of fives.

THE WHISKY RING

Soon received his attention, and the battle he fought with this powerful combination, which claimed, with some show of reason, to be stronger than the Government, has constituted the principal part and the best part of the history of the country during the past year. All the evils of a vicious and corrupting system of civil service had reached a climax in the whiskey ring. Their method of robbing the public was so convenient and simple, and the profits so enormous, that there had grown up within a few years an organized band of politicians and distillers in various parts of the country, whose business it was to systematically defraud the Government, and with a portion of the proceeds to manipulate conventions, control nominations and keep their allies in office. Against this formidable and destructive combination Colonel Bristow, backed by the President and inspired by the order "let no guilty person escape," prepared a plan of campaign, not hastily or loosely, but with wise forethought and circumspection. That the members of the whiskey ring possessed great political influence he was well aware. That they had plenty of money he knew, because he knew the source from which they obtained it. That they would resort to perjury to defend themselves and to assail him he was fully assured, because it was only through wholesale perjury that they could evade the revenue laws. How far the blow he proposed to strike would reach he did not know, but since none but rogues could be harmed, it was immaterial whether it struck persons in high position or not. The commotion which ensued upon the first seizure of the crooked distilleries and their books and papers, the exasperation of the scoundrels who had been so long plundering the treasury, the storm of obloquy and threats that assailed the Secretary, the "pressure" brought to bear upon the President to drive Colonel Bristow out of the Cabinet or compel him to desist from his work, the alarm expressed by venal newspapers lest he should damage the party—all this is too fresh in the public memory to need recapitulation. The various wicked and unfounded stories which the baffled conspirators trumped up to blacken his character, and which he met and put down with the vigor and frankness of a manly nature, even if they were worthy of it, are likewise too well remembered to require any restatement. Suffice it to say that he has paralyzed, for the time being, the most desperate band of desperadoes that this era has brought forth. They are now working with redoubled energy to prevent his nomination for the Presidency, expecting as the result to recover their lost opportunities for plunder.

The following are some of the results of the first year's prosecution of the whiskey ring, the raid having begun the first week in May, 1875. The last returns of money for property seized and in process of condemnation are necessarily slow. The final collection of at least a million more than is now being proceeded against is assured :

Value of property seized	$1,500,000
Value of assessments	1,400,000
Suits on official bonds	250,000
Total	$3,150,000

From the above sources the cash turned into the Treasury to May 1, 1876, amounts to $600,000.

Criminal indictments were as follows : Distillers and rectifiers, 95 ; supervisors, 2 ; revenue agents, 5 ; collectors, 2 ; deputy collectors, 8 ; gaugers, 30 ; storekeepers, 15 ; other persons, 19 ; total, 176 ; convictions and pleas of guilty, 110 ; absconded to foreign countries, 12 ; tried and acquitted, 17.

The total expense to the Treasury Department in detecting frauds and preparing cases for the court has not exceeded $25,000.

Colonel Bristow's war against the whiskey ring has been of immense advantage to the public, not only in saving money to the Treasury, but in exposing the night side of politics, and enabling the people to see clearly the danger that threatens the republic. It is no wonder that the honest and right-thinking masses demand that he shall lead them into a better future and a purer political life. If he is now rejected at the behest of ring politicians, what answer shall be rendered to the people for so sinister an act? Will they not say that he was thrown overboard because he had made an honest effort to put a stop to a gigantic fraud? Can the Republican party afford to expose itself to so grave a charge? Two years ago it lost the elections upon smaller provocation, and although there has since been a partial recovery, it is safe to say that this is no time for trifling with public sentiment.

RESTORATION OF SPECIE PAYMENTS.

On the subject of restoring specie payments, Col. Bristow has left nobody in doubt as to his views. He has given them without ambiguity in two successive reports as Secretary of the Treasury. The following extracts from the Report of 1874 not only define his position, but constitute so clear and convincing an argument in favor of specie resumption that it may well be doubted whether anything more forcible has been written by anybody, in either public or private station, during the whole course of the controversy:

"So much has been spoken and written within the last decade, and especially at the last session of Congress, on the financial questions relating to and growing out of our currency system, that further extended discussion of the subject at this time would scarcely seem to be necessary. The opinions entertained and expressed by public men and communities of people, as well as the sense of Congress, as heretofore indicated by the votes of the two houses, must be accepted as one of the factors of the financial problem. Nevertheless, the great and paramount importance of arriving at an ultimate solution of the matter, and of restoring to the Government and the people a sound and stable currency, induces the Secretary to bring the subject again to the attention of Congress, and to ask that decisive steps be now taken by the law-making power for a return to a specie basis.

"To attempt an enumeration of the complicated mischiefs which flow from an unstable or inconvertible currency would carry this report to an inexcusable length, and, after all, would be but a repetition of what has often been said. No nation can long neglect the wholesome maxims, founded on universal experience, that uphold public credit, without suffering financial disturbances and bringing serious consequences upon its people. It will not be denied that the existing issue of legal-tender notes, as a circulating medium, would never have been made except in the great emergency of a war involving no less an issue than the preservation of the nation. Whether the argument in support of the validity of the legal-tender acts be rested on the war powers conferred on the Government by the Constitution or on other provisions of that instrument, it is clear that Congress could not have been induced to pass such acts under any other circumstances than in a time of the most urgent and pressing need, such as a state of war only produces. The most earnest defenders of the power to issue Government obligations, and make them by law legal-tender for all debts, public and private, would scarcely be found to advocate the exercise of the power except under circumstances of extreme necessity, and then only for the time of the emergency. And there is abundant evidence in the debates and proceedings of Congress, and in the statutes themselves, that it was not intended to make the legal-tender notes the permanent currency of the country. The acts authorizing the issue of such notes provided for their conversion into bonds of the United States, bearing interest at the rate of six per centum per annum.

"The act of March 18, 1869, in terms declares that 'the faith of the United States is solemnly pledged to the payment in coin or its equivalent of all obligations of the United States not bearing interest, known as United States notes.' The same act further affirms that 'The United States solemnly pledges its faith to make provision, at the earliest practicable period, for the redemption of the United States notes in coin.'

"The purpose of the act is well expressed in its title, which declares it to be 'An Act to strengthen the public credit,' and that such was the effect of the act cannot be doubted, for it is an unconditional assurance on the part of the Government, not only that its notes shall be paid in coin, but that this shall be done at the earliest practicable period. The faith of the Government could not be more clearly or absolutely pledged than is done by this act of Congress, to say nothing of previous legislation.

         *   *   *   *

" A dollar legal-tender note, such as is now in circulation, is neither more nor less than a promise of the Government to pay a dollar to the bearer, while no express provision is made by law for paying the dollar at any time whatever; nor is there any existing provision for converting it into anything that stands in a tangible ratio to a coin dollar. As far as existing laws go, there is no reason why the legal-tender note of the denomination of a dollar should pass for one cent of gold, except so far as the Government compels creditors to accept it in discharge of obligations to pay money, and obliges the wealth and commerce of the country to adopt it as a medium of exchange. To this may be added, as an element of the value of a legal-tender dollar, the hope that the Government will sometime or other redeem its paper promises according to their import. The universal use of, and reliance upon, such a currency tends to blunt the moral sense and impair the natural self-dependence of the people, and trains them to the belief that the Government' must directly assist their individual fortunes and business, help them in their personal affairs, and enable them to discharge their debts by partial payment. This inconvertible paper currency begets the delusion that the remedy for private pecuniary distress is in legislative measures, and makes the people unmindful of the fact that the true remedy is in greater production and less spending, and that real prosperity comes only from individual effort and thrift. When exchanges are again made in coin, or in a currency convertible into it at the will of the holder, this truth will be understood and acted upon."

In his report for the year 1875, Secretary Bristow resumed the consideration of the same subject in similar terms. He said :

" The circumstances attending the issue of the United States notes now in circulation impose upon the Government a peculiar obligation to provide for their speedy and certain redemption in coin. They were issued in the exercise of a power which can be called into use only in a time of supreme necessity, and were paid out for the support of an army composed of brave and patriotic citizens who had responded to the call of their country in the hour of its extreme peril. To suffer a promise made at such a time, and under such circumstances, to be dishonored by subsequent indifference or non-performance, would be little better than open repudiation, and would affect injuriously our national name and credit.

It is worthy of note that for the most part those who now oppose the redemption of legal-tender notes and who ask for a further issue, and continued an indefinite reissue of the notes now in circulation, were most strenuous in their opposition to such issues during the civil war. The acts authorizing such issues were denounced as in violation of sound principles of finance, and not warranted by the Constitution. Their constitutional validity was resisted at every point and subjected to the test of judicial decision in almost every court in the country, both state and national. The supreme judicial tribunal of the nation upheld the acts as measures of necessity in a time of great exigency; but it has neither decided nor intimated that such power may be exercised by Congress in time of public tranquility. Indeed, it is fairly inferable, from all the court has said in the various cases in which the question has been before it, that the issue of such notes in time of peace is not within the constitutional power of Congress. The language and argument of the court leave no reason to believe that it would sustain the claim of power to increase the volume of such issues, or to reissue such as have been redeemed in obedience to law, when the public exigency no longer exists. Those who opposed such issues at a time of supreme necessity and insist upon further issues when the emergency has passed away, put themselves in the attitude of opposing war measures in the midst of war, and advocating them in a time of profound peace."

GENERAL CHARACTERISTICS.

From the days of Daniel Boone to the present time, Kentucky has been noted for producing stalwart, fearless men, and the sense of personal honor has ever been high among them. This is a tribute which her sister States, irrespective of political bias, are bound to pay her. Among men of this high and unsullied type Col. Bristow ranks with the highest. Nobody can point to aught in his career which does not have the stamp of candor, courage and truth. A scorn of the petty arts of self-advancement marks his career at every step. Low cunning, intrigue, and the various devices by which political and personal ends are too often achieved, are weapons which he does not understand the use of. So far from seeking political advancement, he has sedulously avoided those who have

sought to thrust it upon him, and has refused to give the
slightest assistance in the preparation of any biographical
sketch of himself designed to make the American people better acquainted with his public services. To persons making
inquiries with a view to advancing him in popular regard he
has replied invariably : "I am not a candidate for any office.
If you wish to learn my history you must go to those who
have known me all my life."

It is both strange and humiliating that a contest for the
Presidency should begin with a general demand to know
whether the respective candidates have ever been guilty of
defrauding the people. It is a fact, nevertheless, that this is
one of the first questions put, and that nothing is taken for
granted. The people have grown suspicious of their public
servants, and they now require every scrap of evidence that
can be adduced to show that the men they are asked to vote
for are not fitter for trial by a petit jury than for the suffrages
of their fellow-citizens. If any candidate shows a backward-
ness in submitting to investigation of his conduct or record,
it is assumed that he desires to conceal something, and that
he is no better than he should be. No man can be expected
to prove a negative, but it may be safely assumed that no
person holding the office which Secretary Bristow holds would
have made the kind of war which he has made on rascals of
high and low degree, if there had been any weak points in his
armor. The whiskey ring have been ransacking his record,
both public and private, for a twelvemonth, and they have produced nothing which shows a stain upon his character, but on the
contrary have brought his noble qualities into clearer light and
more general recognition. They have proved most of all that
he possesses the quality of moral courage, than which nothing
is more conspicuously wanting or more sorely needed in the
public life of America to-day. They have shown that Col.
Bristow, in the path of duty, is impervious alike to cajolery
and threats, that he is not to be turned aside by "influence," nor shaken from his purpose by the clamor of "danger
to the party." All his steps have been those of a massive and
well balanced mind, seeing clearly the object to be attained,
and trampling down the obstacles in his pathway without fear

and without remorse. By pursuing this impartial and unvary-
ing campaign against corruption he has strengthened the party
where it was growing weak, and brought back to allegiance
thousand of voters who had been driven by despair of any improvement in their own party, into the ranks of the enemy.
Many of the latter are now waiting to see whether the reforms
introduced by Secretary Bristow are to be ratified by the Republican party in convention assembled, and continued here after
in the administration, not only of the treasury, but of all other
departments of the government. If Col. Bristow is nominated
they will ask no other assurance. He is the platform for 1876,
and the people require no other. The Southern States, with
but one or two exceptions, have been lost to the Republican
party, and any attempt to carry them by intimidation or coer-
cion will drive away more voters than it will gain. Indiana,
Ohio, New York, Connecticut, New Jersey, California and Wis-
consin are doubtful States, to lose which is to lose the election.
The nomination of Col. Bristow will secure them all, because
he is identified in the minds of the people with the reform of
public abuses. It is an open secret that he favors retrench-
ment and economy in all branches of the public business, reform in the general administration of the government, and the
establishment of the civil service on a basis which will lift it
out of the disrepute into which it has fallen, and make it a
matter of national pride instead of national reproach.

PERSONAL.

In person Col. Bristow is six feet in height, well proportioned,
and weighs 225 pounds. He has an open, frank expression of
countenance and a modest but courteous and prepossessing
manner. The impression he makes upon strangers is that of
a man with a clear eye, a stout heart and a tranquil con-
science. He is the picture of good health, and would attract
notice in a crowd as one having an enormous reserve of physical and mental strength. Finally he is happily married to a
most accomplished and amiable wife, by whom he has had two
children, a daughter and son, both living and both giving every
promise of future worth and usefulness. Col. Bristow

has been equal and more than equal to every station he has been called to fill, in peace and war. If elected President of the United States, he will fill the measure of the public demands of the centennial year by bringing us up to a higher plane of official morality, and thus restoring our prestige among the nations of the world. Having been faithful over a few things, "let him be made master over many."

APPENDIX.

While no one, as has been shown, has been more active than Col. Bristow in repressing violence in the South by the employment of force, no one has labored more effectively to persuade the people of that section to accept the results of the war in good faith and to bring their laws into harmony with the recent amendments to the Constitution. The following selections from his public speeches, made at a time when the State of Kentucky was still sullen and unsatisfied, show how fully his heart was in the great work which he had inherited from his ancestors, and for which he had fought at Donaldson and Shiloh :

[Extract from Col. Bristow's speech at Louisville, July, 1871.]

KENTUCKY BOURBONISM.

" Looking into the constitution of our State, it [the Republican party] finds there whole sections that should have no place in a fundamental law designed for the guidance and government of a great commonwealth of this day. Accepting the fact that 'war legislates,' and acquiescing in the changes that have occurred by the approval of some, and in spite of the opposition of others, the Republican party of Kentucky now unite in demanding that the constitution and laws of our State be adapted to the living requirements of the people, in whose interest all laws should be made. Having neither desire nor ability to carry on perpetual strife with our neighboring sister States, or with the aggregate power of the people of all the States represented in our general government, we insist upon bringing our laws into harmonious relations with theirs. The present constitution of Kentucky was formed and adopted more than twenty years ago, at a time when the *summum bonum* of all political sagacity and so-called statesmanship was the perpetuation of human bondage. Under the influence of this idea every possible safeguard was thrown around the institution of slavery, and the people were practically deprived of the power to modify their own constitution. Intelligent men of this day must be startled to find in the third section of the miscalled bill of rights—a part of our present constitution—that absurd political dogma which announces that 'the right of property is before and higher than any constitutional sanction ; and the right of the owner of a slave to such slave and its increase is the same, and as inviolable as the right of the owner of any property whatever.'

"Always unsound as a political axiom, no argument is necessary to prove the monstrous absurdity of such a declaration at this day, when slavery has no foothold on this continent, and when even the most obdurate of the two classes of Democrats concede that it can never again exist here. But this is not all. Article ten of the present constitution of this State contains three sections, all of which relate solely to the subject of slaves, and that part of the once servile race known as free negroes.

"The second section of the article is as follows :

"'The general assembly *shall* pass laws providing that any free negro or mulatto hereafter immigrating to, and any slave hereafter emancipated in, and refusing to leave this State, or having left, shall return and settle within this State, shall be deemed guilty of *felony* and punished by confinement in the penitentiary thereof.'

"The moral sense of many of the people of Kentucky was shocked by the refinement of cruelty that suggested this section, but the behests of slavery required its adoption, and opposition to it was worse than vain. Every member of the Legislature of Kentucky is required to take an oath to support the constitution, of which this section is a part ; and under its provision it becomes the sworn duty of each member to see that laws are passed for punishing as felons every free negro or mulatto immigrating to this State. The section is imperative and mandatory. It leaves nothing to the discretion of the Legislature. To say that this section has become obsolete by reason of the amendments to the National Constitution, or that the enlightened judgment of mankind forbids its enforcement *now*, is no answer to the objection to its remaining in our printed constitution.

"We have a right to demand, and do demand, that all obsolete and defunct provisions be stricken from our constitution, and that that instrument be made up of living words and sections, adapted to the practical wants of an active, moving and progressive people.

"Nor is this all. Section 8 of article 2 of our present constitution prescribes the qualification of voters, and limits the exercise of the franchise to ' free white male citizens.' By the ratification of the Fifteenth Article of Amendment to the Constitution of the United States, this section of our State constitution is abrogated, and it, too, should be swept from the book. In a word, every provision of that instrument inserted in the interest of slavery—and there are many such—should be expunged, and a new constitution formed in the interest of freedom."

EDUCATION.

" The subject of education is one of vital importance to the people of this State. The Democratic party has shown itself incapable of bringing our State up to the standard of our neighboring States. That party which feeds upon the prejudices of the past, and lives by the petty hates of the present, has not only spurned and neglected the colored race entirely, but it has fallen far short of duty to the white race.

" Our system of common schools, outside the city of Louisville, and possibly one or two others of our smaller cities, is positively discreditable to the State. Indeed, he is guilty of using a misnomer who calls it a system. From the mouth of the Sandy to the Mississippi river it is a blunder and a failure. There are hundreds, yea, thousands, of white children in this Commonwealth who have practically no opportunity to receive a common-school education. Time will not permit me now to stop and point out the many defects and fatal errors in this so-called system. It is sufficient to look over the State and see results. The moral and physical greatness of a State do not depend solely, or even chiefly, upon soil or climate, or even numbers of population. First of all in importance is the development and expansion of intellectual and moral wealth. To this end education of its youth is indispensable. Education adds to the wealth-producing power of the population ; it increases wages twenty-five per cent. in ordinary cases, and under favorable circumstances often much more. The value of the citizen to the community at large and his power as a producer to add to the common stock of wealth are very materially enhanced by education. The increase of value and power arises from causes so obvious and well known that they need not be enumerated. Ignorance and vice too often go hand in hand. An educated population is far less liable than an uneducated and ignorant one to become an expense to the State through poverty and crime.

" If we turn to the statistics for 1860, the latest we have on this subject, it will be found that Kentucky had at that time 419,169 free adults, of whom 73,522, or 17.54 per cent., were illiterate—that is, unable to read or write. Thus we see that more than one-sixth, almost one-fifth, of the entire free adult population was unable to read or write in 1860. This does not include white children or the colored population, then slaves. If we add to this number the then adult slave population, 91,330, we have a total adult population, white and black, of 510,490, of which 32 per cent., or nearly one-third of our entire adult population, was illiterate in 1860. Turning to the great State north of us we find of their adult population, white and black, the per cent. of illiterate as follows : Ohio, 6.12 ; Indiana, 11 ; Illinois, 8 ; Iowa, 7 ; Kansas, 6.

"All these are newer States than Kentucky, and the youngest man before me remembers well when some of them emerged from the chrysalis condition of Territories and put on the habiliments of States. No thoughtful man who loves his State, and who fondly cherishes the dream of her future greatness, can refrain from asking the question, Why is all this so ? To the mind not seared by prejudice, or blinded by hate, the answer is easy, and suggests itself. It is because in Kentucky we have many politician and but few statesmen. It is because, with our people, politics is a mere sentiment and not the science of government, which looks to the aggregate good of the masses and the augmentation of the strength of the State.

"The voice of civilization cries aloud against this state of things. The welfare of our State and the highest interests of society require that facilities for acquiring a common English education be placed within the reach of every child of the Commonwealth, white and black. The idle clamor against mixed schools does not relieve us of the duty that rests upon us. The necessities of the situation demand school-houses and school-teachers for all, but not mixed schools. If it be the desire of one or both races to have separate schools, be it so ; but in the name of our high and sacred duty to see that the Commonwealth suffers no injury, and that the best interests of society are cared for, let us make free schools *for all.* If I am asked how it is proposed to raise the money to defray the expenses of such schools, I answer, *by taxing the property of the State. I would tax the rich man's property to educate his poor neighbor's child. I would tax the white man's property to educate the black man's child, and vice versa. In a word, I would tax all the property of the State to educate all the children of the State."*

MISSION OF THE REPUBLICAN PARTY.

"The mission of the Republican party is not yet ended. The loyal people of this country who preserved the government in war and have maintained its honor in peace are not yet ready to hand it over to the party that conspired to destroy it, and has resisted every effort to make it indestructible.

"At no time in our history has the cause of civil and religious liberty made such progress as in the decade under the fostering care of the Republican party. In giving freedom with civil and political rights to one race, it has not been unmindful of the rights and liberties of the other. The same constitutional provision that gave freedom to the black man makes it forever impossible to enslave any portion of the white race.

" The citizenship secured by the fourteenth article of amendment to all persons born or naturalized in the United States applies alike to all persons, rich and poor, white and black. The inhibition upon the States to make or enforce any law which shall abridge the privileges or immunities of citizens of the United States, or to deprive any person of life, liberty or property without due process of law, or to deny to any person within their jurisdiction the equal protection of the laws, is a bulwark of safety to every citizen and a protection against the oppressions that might otherwise arise from sectional jealousy and local hate. The constitutional guarantee of the elective franchise is applicable to all races of people, and henceforth neither the United States nor any State can deny or abridge this inestimable right on account of race, color or previous condition. All these constitutional provisions were passed in the interest of personal liberty and individual security. ' The love of liberty is inherent in human nature. It may be stifled, but not without much difficulty. Easy to be wrought upon as well as powerful and active, whenever it is not gratified there is danger to the State. Gratify it, and you secure the safety of society.'

"Neither these constitutional provisions nor any statute passed in pursuance of them oppresses or harms any human being. The penalties of the civil rights and Ku Klux acts are aimed solely at the lawless and violent. No peaceful citizen or law abiding community has apprehension of injury or oppression from them. A government which cannot protect its humblest citizen from outrage and injury is unworthy the name, and ought not to command the support of a free people. But ' the wicked flee when no man pursueth,' and when you hear these statutes denounced by Democratic speakers, you may be sure that either they or their friends have committed or are likely to commit the crimes for which the punishment is provided.

" These are the works of the great Republican party of the nation, which saved the country in war, and is able to preserve it in peace. This is the party that must control the destinies of this free country for years to come. May we not confidently appeal to the young men of Kentucky who propose to live in the stirring present and to be actors in the coming future, to cut loose from the hurtful prejudices of the past and take part in the great work of wheeling our State into the line of progress and advancing it in the race for prosperity and material wealth.

" Sooner or later the cloud that now hangs over Kentucky and obstructs the moral vision of her people must vanish like a morning's mist before the rising sun of a brighter and better civilization."

ORATION AT CAVE HILL CEMETERY.

Five years later Col. Bristow was called to deliver the oration at Cave Hill Cemetery, near Louisville, over the graves of his companions in arms, on Decoration Day, May 29, 1875. This oration is imbued with such lofty patriotism and solemn truth, and is so wisely adapted to the condition of the South and of the whole Union at the present time, that the compilers of this biographical notice deem it the most fitting conclusion of their task.

ADDRESS.

" Perhaps nothing more distinctly marks the degree of civilization attained by a country or community than tender regard for the memory of its dead. The monuments erected, the flowers planted by loving hands in the resting places of the dead, testify to the virtues of the living. The splendid cemeteries of great cities, and the modest graveyards of villages and neighborhoods, betoken the existence of a sentiment alike creditable to each. Our own beautiful Cave Hill, wherein we meet to-day, with its green sward, its trees and flowers, its marble monuments, bearing names familiar to us all, tells how the people of Louisville cherish the memory of departed friends. But our solemn and tender feeling for the dead is here exalted by the generous spirit of patriotism, inspired by recollections which the ceremonies of this day must revive. We are assembled to celebrate the valor and virtue of men who died to preserve the blessings of personal liberty and free government to us and our posterity. The memory of their heroic endurance and daring courage should live in the hearts of succeeding generations, so long as the principles for which they fought and died shall survive, and be valued among men.

" Occasions like this must ever be full of interest to those who love their country and desire the perpetuation of its free institutions. With mingled feelings of sadness and joy we come to decorate with fresh flowers, emblematic of our affection, the graves of the soldiers who gave their lives in defense of that Union which was preserved by the valor of themselves and their comrades ; nor are we alone in the performance of this sacred and patriotic duty. In all parts of the country this day is devoted to the commemoration of the patriotism and courage of those who fell in a struggle which the world can never forget. Although ten years have passed since the conflict, it is even now too soon to know and appreciate to their fullest extent its beneficial results, or its influence upon the destiny of a great people. For the purposes and duty of this day, it is enough to know that they who sleep beneath this sod battled and died for a country which still survives to shed its blessings upon them. By the united efforts of themselves and their surviving comrades, the Government for which they went forth to battle has not only been saved from overthrow, but its foundations made deeper and broader. The fundamental idea upon which the great founders builded has been carried to its logical result.

" The political axiom of our fathers, ' that all men are created equal ; that they are endowed, by their Creator, with certain inalienable rights ; that among these are life, liberty, and the pursuit of happiness,' has found fuller illustration and broader application.

" This immortal declaration is no longer limited by ideal boundaries, but reaches forth to every man, of whatever race or color, who breathes the air or treads the soil of the Union. The universality of its application is now plainly declared in our written Constitution, and our national emblem floats over none who are not entitled to its equal protection. Looking back to the beginning of the struggle, and calling to mind the declared purposes with which the Government entered upon it, the results achieved may well excite the special wonder of the civilized world. At first, engaging in a war of self-defense, the Government undertook to repossess its own property, and to assert its rightful authority in disputed places. It was regarded by most persons as little more than a trial of the strength of free government. For a time the battle was uncertain ; to many the issue seemed doubtful. Despondency lowered over the land, and gloomy forebodings filled the hearts of patriots. Political intrigue, and the clashing of personal ambitions, well nigh destroyed at least one of our greatest armies. But amid the reverses in arms and the wrangling of politicians, the valor of the soldiery never faltered, and in His own good time God raised up for us great military leaders, who were equal to the emergency, and who, having no political ends to subserve, and no selfish ambition to gratify, led our gallant armies to final victory. Meanwhile the delays and postponements, resulting from the causes referred to, had furnished time and opportunity for thoughtful consideration of the questions underlying the conflict. The man who then stood at the helm of State, by the choice of the people, and who, by the Constitution, was commander-in-chief of the army and navy, had declared in 1858, with scarcely less than prophetic vision, that this Government could not endure permanently half slave and half free. As the struggle progressed, the truth of this announcement forced itself upon the people. The men of the South, who were in arms against the authority of the Government, had avowed their purpose to build up a separate government, with slavery for its corner-stone. The irrepressible conflict between freedom and slavery had now begun in earnest, and the people of the adhering States, at first reluctantly and slowly, but at last firmly, resolved that slavery and the rebellion should perish together, and to-day they sleep in a common grave.

"He who fails to see in all this the hand of an all-wise Providence is but a dull reader of events. And who, in all this broad land, will now avow a desire for a different result? Speaking upon the soil of one of the late slave States, I but declare a truth, which will not be controverted or questioned by any considerable number of intelligent persons, when I assert that a great blight has been removed from the South by the abolition of slavery. It requires no prophet to foretell that sooner or later the South must enter upon a career of unexampled prosperity under the influence of free institutions. Her resources are, practically, boundless. Her fertile soil, her rich mineral deposits, her propitious climate, all point to future wealth and power. Free labor must, and will, develop these, as it has already done in the less favored region of the North. The causes which have operated since the close of the civil war to retard the onward movement and check the prosperity of the South might be easily traced, but this is not a suitable occasion to discuss them.

"If I am asked when will this predicted prosperity be realized, my answer is, when the passions and prejudices engendered by the strife shall have entirely subsided; when the inalienable right of every man to equal freedom with every other man is fully recognized by society; when the laborer is not only fully protected in life, liberty and the pursuit of happiness, but ample provision is made for the education of his children; and when it becomes known and accepted that wealth and intellectual improvement come only from individual industry and effort, and not from the pursuit of what we call

politics. Then, and not till then, will the South have entered
upon the full realization of the benefits which must eventually
flow from the change. No political economist will deny that
educated labor brings greater rewards both to the employer
and the employed; hence, considerations of self-interest, to
say nothing of the duty required of us by the golden rule,
demand the education of all the people. In view, then, of
what has been already achieved, and of what remains to be
surely realized hereafter as the results of the war, which
peopled the graves that lie before us, have we not great occasion to pour out the gratitude of our hearts with the flowers
now strewn on this consecrated spot?

"The ceremonies of to-day tend to keep alive the sentiments
of patriotism in the hearts of the survivors of those whose
virtues we commemorate. The very performance of this duty
of affection towards the dead has had its reflex influence upon
the living. Here we are reminded that the strength of the
Government under which we live is in the loyalty and virtue of
its people; that the citizens are the country, and the country
is what the people make it. This is the key that opens the
secret of the strength of republican government, which leans
upon the people, and not the people upon it. The whole story
of the patriotism and sacrifices of the men who died in defense
of the Union was told by Mr. Lincoln when he declared on the
field of Gettysburg that they gave their lives that 'government
of the people, by the people, and for the people, should not
perish from the earth.' A nobler sentiment, in fitter words,
was never uttered.

"These ceremonies are conducted in no spirit of boastful
exultation over the men who fell on the other side, or their
surviving comrades. The graves throughout the South, in
which sleep thousands who arrayed themselves against the
Government, testify to their courage and soldierly bearing.
Their bravery and endurance were illustrated on many well-con-
tested fields. It is impossible to doubt that the masses among
them fought for what they believed to be right, and however
they may have been misled by false theories of government, or
deluded by the artful teachings of cunning and ambitious
leaders, we cannot fail to recognize their valor, or the tenacity
and fidelity with which they adhered to the cause in which
they had enlisted, so long as the conflict continued. If our
own great President could declare in the midst of the strife
that it was prosecuted on our part 'with malice toward none,
but with charity for all,' how much more ready should we be
to bury the animosities that belong to the past, and concede to
the men who fought against us the qualities illustrated by their
courage and devotion to the cause espoused by them? Who

that bears in his bosom the heart of an American citizen can fail to recall with proud satisfaction the many acts of kindness and liberality of our military leaders towards a fallen foe? No incident of the war will bear a more conspicuous place in history than that which occurred at the crowning victory at Appomattox, where our greatest military chieftain accorded to the conquered army of the rebellion terms of surrender which were both just and generous. For his superb magnanimity, for his steadfast and unselfish patriotism, no less than for his splendid achievements in the field, the people have twice called him to preside over a reunited country, and in spite of political enmity and personal malice, harmless against such as he, history will accord him the highest rank as a leader.

"The two grand results of the war, which more than compensate the country for all its sad bereavements and vast expenditure and waste of money and property, are the extinction of slavery and the recognized indissolubility of our National Union; and the time is not far distant when these will be accepted and admitted as blessings by the people of every section. Men of the South will, sooner or later, admit that success in what they undertook would have been a grievous misfortune, even to themselves. What they may think of their action in the past is of little moment, so far as it can affect the present and future interests of the country. What we have a right to expect and insist upon is practical loyalty in the future to the country, and cheerful obedience to its Constitution and laws. Mere historical and sentimental loyalty is of far less consequence. We ask no sacrifice of conviction, no humiliation of soldierly pride, while insisting on and enforcing every principle resulting from the victory. We may look with indulgence, if not with indifference, on the apologies and defenses that will certainly, through all time, be put forth by the descendants of the men who fought on the side of the rebellion, and agree to differ with them on what is rapidly becoming a mere chronicle of record and of theory. The history of the world furnishes examples from which we may learn lessons of wisdom in this respect. The past struggles in our mother country illustrate what I mean. The great leaders on each side of the civil war of the seventeenth century, Hampden, Pym and Cromwell, Falkland, Hyde and Ormond, have full justice done them by all competent historians, and their virtues and talents are the common heritage of the English people; and the historians of those times are equally loyal to the British constitution of to-day, whether they take the side of the Cavaliers or espouse the cause of the Roundheads. Nay, more, in the next generation after the termination of that bitter and bloody struggle, the immediate descendants of the men whom I have mentioned, and who probably could not have discussed the question of the arrest of the five members of the Grand Remonstrance without crossing swords, united in driving James the Second from the throne and establishing that combination of freedom and order which has given England her greatest prosperity. The Scottish rebellion in favor of the House of Stuart, in the last century, is a still more striking illustration of how men may hold totally different and irreconcilable views on historical issues, and yet be practically and earnestly loyal to the present and future of a common country. As a writer of history and historical romance, Sir Walter Scott was an intense Jacobite and a bitter opponent to the House of Hanover, and yet, in spite of historical theories, he was an enthusiastic loyalist towards George the Third and George the Fourth. No part of the British Isle was more loyal than Scotland, and yet I undertake to say, that to-day in no part of the civilized world could there be aroused more bitter discussions and controversies over the struggles in which that people have been engaged.

" May we not, then, look forward with assured confidence to the time, in the near future, when all intelligent men, North and South, will not only accept the results of the late conflict, but will recognize the blessings that flow from it, and admit that any other issue would have been an irreparable calamity to both sections of the country. While we must differ from those who sought to dissolve the Union and look from a different standpoint upon the history of the struggle that ensued, we may safely concede to them the right to hold such opinions as they like in respect of the past, and claim from them only a cheerful and hearty loyalty to the present and future. And why should this not be so? Are we not bound together by ties of consanguinity and community of material interests? Whatever promotes discord, or weakens our common government, threatens danger and disaster to all alike, and whatever gives strength and perpetuity to our free institutions promises blessings to the people in every part of the country, and to their posterity.

" God speed the time when the men of the North and of the South shall vie with each other in efforts to rebuild the waste places, to promote the general welfare and to advance by all proper means the greatness and prosperity of our common country !"